DEAD COOL

BY PETER CLOVER

ILLUSTRATED BY BRANN GARVEY

Librarian Reviewer
Marci Peschke
Librarian, Dallas Independent School District
MA Education Reading Specialist, Stephen F. Austin State University
Learning Resources Endorsement, Texas Women's University

Reading Consultant
Elizabeth Stedem
Educator/Consultant, Colorado Springs, CO
MA in Elementary Education, University of Denver, CO

▼▼ STONE ARCH BOOKS
Minneapolis   San Diego

First published in the United States in 2007
by Stone Arch Books,
151 Good Counsel Drive, P.O. Box 669,
Mankato, Minnesota 56002.
www.stonearchbooks.com

Published by arrangement with
Barrington Stoke Ltd, Edinburgh.

Library of Congress Cataloging-in-Publication Data
Clover, Peter.
    Dead cool / by Peter Clover; illustrated by Brann Garvey.
    p. cm. — (Pathway Books)
    Summary: Sammy's new pet, a parrot named Polly, is quite boring, but
the friends she attracts—another parrot and a ghostly pirate crew—prove to
be very exciting.
    ISBN-13: 978-1-59889-100-3 (hardcover)
    ISBN-10: 1-59889-100-6 (hardcover)
    ISBN-13: 978-1-59889-254-3 (paperback)
    ISBN-10: 1-59889-254-1 (paperback)
    [1. Parrots—Fiction. 2. Ghosts—Fiction. 3. Pirates—Fiction.] I. Garvey,
Brann, ill. II. Title. III. Series.
PZ7.C62475Dea 2007
[Fic]—dc22   2006007172

Art Director: Heather Kindseth
Cover Graphic Designer: Brann Garvey
Interior Graphic Designer: Kay Fraser

1 2 3 4 5 6 11 10 09 08 07 06

Printed in the United States of America

TABLE OF CONTENTS

CHAPTER 1

PRETTY POLLY

Sammy wanted a dog. He wanted a dog very badly.

Sammy didn't want just any old dog. His dog had to be a huge Great Dane.

Sammy's mom said, "No way!"

She told Sammy he couldn't have a dog at all, not even a little dog.

The problem was that Sammy and his parents lived in a very small apartment.

Their apartment was on the third floor of an old house that sat right on the edge of the sea.

On the first floor, Mr. Hackbone sold all sorts of interesting and old things in his store.

"We can't keep a dog up here in the apartment!" said Mom. "We don't have a yard. Dogs need yards. Dogs dig. It wouldn't be right."

She shook her head and added, "Anyway, Mr. Hackbone would not like it if we had a dog!"

"A cat, then!" begged Sammy. He looked at his mom. "How about a big old tomcat? Cats don't need yards. Lots of people keep cats in apartments. Cats love small spaces. Ask anyone!"

"Not a cat," said Dad. He shook his head and crossed his arms. "Never! Cats have sharp claws. A cat would rip up this place in ten seconds. How about a nice goldfish?"

"Boring," said Sammy. "I'd get dizzy watching it swim around and around all day. So dizzy that I'd faint."

He fell to the floor with his eyes rolling around.

"Okay. What about a bird? A parakeet, maybe?" asked Mom.

"Parakeets aren't cool. They're too small," Sammy told her. "How about an ostrich? Or an eagle?"

In the end they chose a parrot. A bright, green, talking parrot.

Dad went out and picked up the parrot the very next day.

Mr. Hackbone didn't mind that they had a parrot in the apartment. He even gave Mom an old brass birdcage. He told them he had found the birdcage in the cellar under the store.

The cage was great, but the parrot was no good at all. It didn't even talk! What good was a parrot that couldn't talk? Not a peep! Not a squawk! Zilch! Nothing!

"I thought this parrot was supposed to talk!" Sammy complained.

"Give Polly time," said Mom. "Let her get used to us and the apartment. I'm sure she'll have lots to say in a day or two."

Mom pushed out her lips and blew kisses to the bird through the bars of the cage.

Polly fluffed up her feathers. Then she leaned back so far that she fell off her perch.

She swung upside down and landed with her head in the seed tray.

"This bird is crazy," said Sammy. He rolled his eyes and looked away. "She can't even stay on her perch. Some parrot she is!"

Polly dropped to the floor of her cage, got up, and began to scratch around in the grit and sawdust.

Sammy popped a grape through the bars and watched Polly kick it around like a football.

Then she picked it up and peeled it with her beak. Polly liked grapes.

"Clever Polly," said Sammy. The parrot looked at him with her beady black eyes.

Then she gave out a loud squawk!

"Pretty Polly. Pretty Polly," squawked Sammy.

The parrot put her head to one side and waited for another grape.

After nine grapes, Sammy gave up.

Except for a few squawks, when Polly saw herself in the mirror, she never said anything.

Mom smiled. "Give her time," she said. "I think she's just shy."

But three days passed and Polly hadn't said a word.

The next day, a Thursday, Sammy came stomping up the stairs to the apartment and crashed into the small living room.

He threw his school bag across the room and onto the couch.

"Pretty birdie," said a voice from behind him.

It was a squawky parrot voice, and it came from the corner of the room where Polly's cage stood.

Sammy spun around. Could it be true? Had Polly finally spoken?

Sammy dashed across the room and looked into the cage. He gasped.

There, sitting on the perch, was not just one bright green parrot, but two!

CHAPTER 2

A Feathered Phantom

"Wow!" said Sammy.

At first he thought that Mom and Dad had brought another parrot home.

But when he looked closer, Sammy was in shock.

There was something very odd about this second parrot.

It seemed to be there, but it didn't look exactly like a real parrot. It looked more like a fuzzy picture of a parrot.

When Sammy stared hard at the parrot, he could see right through it.

Polly was thrilled. She was gripping her perch so hard that her eyes almost popped out. The second parrot snuggled up to her and cooed as he said Polly's name over and over again.

"Polly, Polly. Pretty Polly. Pretty Polly," said the new parrot.

Sammy's parrot was shy. This new one was bold and was a showoff.

"Pretty Polly. Who's a pretty Polly, then? Phwoaarrhh!" The new parrot loudly squawked again and again.

Sammy opened his mouth but no sound came out. He wanted to say something, but before he could form his words, the second parrot disappeared.

A silver mist floated and twisted upward through the bars of the cage.

Poof!

The other parrot was gone.

Sammy didn't tell anyone. That night he couldn't sleep. He kept getting up, creeping into the living room, and checking on Polly.

"I've got to figure this out!" Sammy whispered to himself.

Was it all a dream? Had he really seen a second parrot? And was that other parrot really a ghost?

Tired and worn out, Sammy fell into a deep sleep.

Morning came. Mom yelled from the kitchen, "Sammy, breakfast!"

Sammy jumped out of bed and ran into the living room. Polly was in her cage. The ghost parrot was sitting right next to her.

The new parrot sat so close that he pushed Polly up against the side of the cage until her feathers stuck out through the bars.

Sammy rubbed his eyes. Was he dreaming? No. The other parrot was still there. This was cool. Dead cool!

"Where did you come from?" asked Sammy softly, so that his mom wouldn't hear.

"Captain Crabmeat's a clever boy," squawked the parrot, looking at Polly. "Polly, Polly. Pretty Polly. Give us a kiss, me darling!"

This parrot could really talk. It was amazing! And it had a great name, Captain Crabmeat!

Mom called again from the kitchen. When Sammy spun around, he saw a monster cat. A huge, red tomcat rested in the armchair.

"A cat!" Sammy exclaimed.

Could this be true? Sammy shivered. He saw the cat's fuzzy red fur.

Like the second parrot, the cat was a hazy ghost. But it was there! Sammy could see it as plain as day.

"Sammy!" Mom called again. "Breakfast! Now!"

Sammy took one more look at the cat before he went to the kitchen.

He had just sat down at the table when the cat came into the kitchen after him. It jumped up and settled on his lap. Sammy felt the cat's warm body against his legs.

Sammy stroked the soft, red fur.

Mom and Dad said nothing. It was clear that they couldn't see the cat.

Just like the parrot, the cat could only be seen by Sammy.

"Shiver me timbers. Polly, Polly. Pretty, pretty Polly," Captain Crabmeat was squawking loudly in the next room.

But Mom and Dad acted as if they didn't hear a thing!

Sammy quickly ate his breakfast and got ready for school. He left the red cat asleep on his bed.

It was really hard to leave the house that morning. Sammy wanted to stay at home and find out what was going on. He wanted to see if the cat would vanish again, like the parrot.

He also wanted to see if anything else would arrive out of thin air.

CHAPTER 3

An Unexpected Visitor

The school day dragged on. It was Friday, and the students were going home early for spring break. All of the students were leaving at 2 p.m.

Sammy ran all the way home. He ran up the stairs to the apartment and let himself in with his key.

Mom worked part-time in Mr. Hackbone's shop. She wouldn't come up to the apartment before 3:30 p.m.

Sammy had more than an hour all to himself.

First things first. Sammy dashed into the living room. Polly and Crabmeat were kissing and cuddling in the corner of the parrot cage. Polly seemed to be enjoying herself.

"Polly, Polly. Pretty Polly," squawked Crabmeat as Sammy came into the room. "Land ahoy. Strike up the Jolly Roger. Pieces of eight. Pieces of eight."

Once Crabmeat started to talk, he just wouldn't shut up. Crabmeat seemed to be very excited about something.

All at once, Sammy felt an odd fizzing in the air.

He looked around for the red cat. But the big tomcat wasn't in the living room.

In fact, he couldn't see it anywhere.

Sammy had left his bedroom door open a crack in case the big cat wanted to go for a walk. But that seemed like a bad idea now. After all, if the cat could appear out of thin air, then it could pass through walls and doors anytime it wanted. Sammy checked his room. The cat wasn't there!

Maybe it's in the kitchen, Sammy thought. But it wasn't. He looked everywhere in the small apartment, then gave up and went back to his room again. When he pushed open the door and stepped inside, Sammy gasped.

There, lying on his bed, was not just one cat, but two huge toms, one red and one striped. And there was something else.

Sitting in a chair was a boy. He was flipping through Sammy's sports magazines.

Sammy was amazed. The boy dropped the magazines and stared back at Sammy from across the room.

This boy was about the same age as Sammy, but he was pale gray all over. Sammy could see right through him. The boy wore shabby trousers and a tattered shirt. His hair was long and pulled back in a ponytail. His bare feet were grubby. A smell of salt and seaweed floated from the boy's corner of the room.

The boy spoke first.

"Ahoy, shipmate!" He sounded bright and cheerful.

Unlike Sammy, this boy didn't seem at all shocked.

"My name's Smitty. Welcome aboard," he added with a grin.

Sammy was stunned. "Hi," was all he could say.

"Strike up the Jolly Roger," Crabmeat squawked from the living room. "Pieces of eight. Pieces of eight."

Smitty laughed and so did Sammy. The crazy parrot seemed to have broken the spell.

"Where the heck did you come from?" Sammy said at last. "What are you doing here in my room?"

Sammy didn't mean to sound so rude. It just sort of came out that way.

Sammy hoped that he hadn't upset the boy. After all, it was quite a shock for Sammy to find a ghost sitting in his room.

He could see that Smitty was upset. The bright, cheerful grin faded. It was as if his light had gone out.

"Sorry!" said Smitty. "I didn't think you'd mind if I dropped in."

Then he closed his eyes and faded into thin air. All that remained was a faint smell of the sea.

"Come back!" yelled Sammy. "It's all right. Come back! You can stay. I want you to stay."

But the boy didn't come back.

The boy was gone.

Sammy spun around to face the bed. The two cats were gone, too!

Sammy ran into the living room. Polly sat alone on her perch. She looked confused and upset.

"Pretty Polly. Pretty Polly." It was the first time that Polly had ever spoken. Sadness filled her voice. Even Crabmeat was gone!

CHAPTER 4

"SHIVER ME TIMBERS!"

At exactly 3:30 p.m., Sammy's mom came up from working at Mr. Hackbone's shop.

Right away, she sent Sammy out to buy bread and milk at Super Shopper.

Sammy slowly went out. While he walked, he thought about Smitty and the other strange events of the past few days.

Sammy wished that he'd been kinder to the ghost in his room. Would the boy ever come back? He might.

After all, Crabmeat already came back twice!

Sammy still didn't tell his parents about the ghosts' visits. They would think he had made up the whole story because they couldn't see anything.

After all, everyone knows that ghosts aren't real!

On the way back from Super Shopper, Sammy stopped on the sidewalk and looked up at the apartment windows. Then he studied the front of the house.

It was like seeing the house for the first time. The house was very, very old.

But just how old was it? Sammy wondered.

The crooked windows of Mr. Hackbone's shop had tiny glass panes. Four numbers were carved above the door. It looked like a date: 1758.

Wow! The house was really old!

Sammy had never noticed the date before. He wanted to know more, so he decided to ask Mr. Hackbone about it in the morning. But that night something even stranger happened!

Sammy was sitting in bed that night, reading his magazines, when his nose started to twitch.

The smell of fish and seaweed floated into his room.

He took a long, deep sniff. When he looked up, he gasped. Smitty, the ghost boy, stood at the end of his bed. Sammy was shocked, but pleased.

The two big cats had come back too, and were padding around on his bed. They plopped themselves down on his soft pillows.

Then Sammy heard Crabmeat squawking next door.

"Hello!" Sammy said softly to Smitty. This time he was careful to sound nice and friendly. "I'm sorry about what happened the last time you were here. I'm glad you came back!"

Sammy wanted to talk and find out why Smitty came to see him. It was all so weird.

Smitty grinned. "I hope you don't mind," he said. His eyes shined. "But I've got a few more friends with me."

What did he mean? Before Sammy had time to ask, eleven sailors from the good ship *Black Crow* stepped through his bedroom walls.

A strong smell of fish and the sea floated through his room. Somewhere Sammy could hear creaking sounds like those of an old ship. He stared hard at the pirate crew. That's what they were, pirates!

Bacon the ship cook, Doc Bones, Squire Delaney, and Boris the officer all stood before Sammy. The seven deck hands wore funny clothes with cutoff pants and flashy shirts. Sammy couldn't believe his eyes!

CHAPTER 5

RED BEARD THE REALLY ROTTEN

Sammy sat up in bed and gazed silently at the sight before him.

"Is it all right if we stay?" asked Smitty. "We won't get in the way. We won't take up any space and no one can see us here except for you and your parrot!"

But what if Mom finds out? thought Sammy. She'd go crazy. She would hit the roof.

She'll want to get rid of them all right away!

It was almost time for bed. Sammy didn't think it would matter if his new visitors stayed for just one night.

He didn't actually tell them it would be okay. He just nodded his head.

Suddenly, the pirate crew started to sing loudly.

"Yo ho ho and a bottle of rum," they sang.

Sammy put a finger into each ear. He was sure his mom and dad would hear all that pirate noise! After all, his parents were in the next room watching TV. He thought for sure they would come rushing into his bedroom. But they didn't.

"My mom and dad can't see or hear ghosts," Sammy said to his ghostly friends.

At last, the crew stopped singing, and sat on Sammy's bed. The amazing thing was that they didn't take up much space at all.

Then the talking began. Sammy told them all about school. But there were so many questions he wanted to ask them. Who were they? Where did they come from? What did they want?

This is what they told Sammy:

Nearly 250 years ago, in a time of sailing ships and pirates, Smitty and his friends were the cabin boy and crew aboard the *Black Crow*. It was a pirate ship that roamed the Seven Seas.

Crabmeat was the *Black Crow*'s lucky mascot. The two big cats were the ship's rat catchers. For years the *Black Crow* sailed the Seven Seas and robbed trading ships.

But the crew didn't want to be outlaws. They wanted to be jolly sailors. They were only pirates because many, many years ago the evil Red Beard the Really Rotten had forced them to become pirates.

Even though the crew was scared stiff of Red Beard the Really Rotten, they planned a mutiny, so they could get rid of Red Beard. They made him walk the plank.

Before Red Beard reached the end of the plank, disaster struck. The ship hit a big rock, and the *Black Crow* sank.

Everyone on board drowned. But that wasn't the end of it. Worse was yet to come. The crew all turned into ghosts.

Ever since, the crew members have roamed the world, unable to rest for fear that Red Beard would catch them. He had been chasing them for almost 250 years.

He wanted his revenge.

"But why have you come here?" Sammy asked. Sammy was starting to get worried. "Won't Red Beard the Really Rotten follow you and come here, too?"

The crew looked around with their shifty eyes.

Smitty spoke. "It was Crabmeat who found the way here through the mist."

"It seemed like a safe place," added Smitty. "Once he made it safely through to your side, we sent the cats. Then I came."

"But we're still not sure how safe it is," said Squire Delaney. "We've never found a hiding place like this before! And we're so tired. We can't keep running forever. We need rest."

Sammy wondered if the old birdcage had something to do with the pirate crew's sudden appearances. He knew that the cage was very old.

He remembered that Mr. Hackbone told Mom the cage had been in his cellar for years.

In fact, it might have been there when the pirates first arrived.

No one seemed to know where the cage came from. But did it matter? The pirate crew members were what mattered now! They were right there, tucked into Sammy's bed.

CHAPTER 6

A Storm Is Brewing

The pirates told wild stories all night long, but finally Sammy fell fast asleep.

He was happy to find his bedroom empty when he woke up the next morning. He felt worn out.

Sammy could smell bacon. He rubbed his eyes. Perhaps last night had just been a big dream!

He would go down to see Mr. Hackbone after breakfast, and ask about the old house and the parrot cage. Was there a link between them?

Sammy pulled on his jeans and a t-shirt. Then he walked barefoot into the kitchen.

The first thing that Sammy saw was Smitty, sitting in his chair at the table. Crabmeat sat on Smitty's shoulder.

Sammy felt something soft and furry against his feet. Looking down, he saw the two huge cats rubbing themselves against his legs.

"Morning, Sam," said Mom. "Breakfast is ready."

She flipped two eggs and some crispy bacon onto a plate.

Smitty licked his lips. He hadn't eaten for years. Not for about 250 years! And he'd never seen bacon like this!

Sammy gave Smitty a nod and a signal to move into the next chair. Then Sammy sat down.

Dad came in with his newspaper and plopped himself down on the other side of the table.

All at once, the crew of the *Black Crow* stepped through the wall behind Dad's chair.

They stood, bending over the table, drooling at Sammy's plate of bacon and eggs.

"Shiver me timbers! Ship ahoy! Pieces of eight! Pieces of eight!"

Crabmeat landed on Sammy and squawked loudly in his ear.

Dad didn't even notice. He just went on reading his newspaper. Mom poured the coffee.

"It's a bit warm in here this morning," she said. "No air."

She flung open the window and looked up at the sky.

"Those clouds over the sea are so black," she said. "A big storm must be coming. Goodness, it's stuffy in here."

I know why, thought Sammy. He didn't say anything.

He just sat there. His face went pale. The air in the apartment did feel thick.

In fact, it felt so thick, you could almost cut it with a knife. Or with a pirate sword.

Sammy didn't eat any of his breakfast. He sensed that Smitty and the pirate crew had something to do with this stuffy feeling and the coming storm.

He stared past his dad to where Smitty stood. Smitty still stared hungrily at the big plate of bacon and eggs.

"This bacon smells funny," said Dad. "A little like seaweed!"

He lifted a whole strip on his fork and took a deep sniff.

The smell of the sea filled the small kitchen. Then the bacon vanished.

Smitty stood, licking his lips.

Crabmeat squawked, and Dad just stared at his empty fork.

Outside, the sky grew darker. All at once, the ghostly crew in the kitchen became restless.

They looked at each other. They were worried. The storm was right above the house.

Sammy's hair stood on end. A deep rumble from behind the black clouds shook the windows, and a flash of lightning lit up the room.

Mom gave a scream. Crabmeat fell off Sammy's shoulder.

Suddenly, Red Beard the Really Rotten appeared at the open kitchen door, wild with rage.

He wore a thick gray coat and an old, real pirate hat. He had one wooden leg and a metal hook in place of a hand. He also wore a cloth patch over his right eye.

It seemed to Sammy that there was quite a lot of him missing. But what was there was very scary.

Nearly 250 years of anger oozed out of every part of his body. Smoke came out of his nose, and red flames crackled from his big, bushy beard.

The ghost of Red Beard the Really Rotten was six feet tall and as wide as a barn door.

Sammy and the pirate ghosts looked at Red Beard with terror. The air popped and fizzed around him.

Red Beard began to grin, an angry grin that flashed like lightning all over his ugly face.

The crew gasped. Smitty's eyes grew as big as plates.

Red Beard glared at his shocked crew. "At last!" he yelled. He smelled like stale fish. "At last! Revenge is mine!"

CHAPTER 7

THE FINAL REVENGE

Mom slammed the kitchen window shut. "What's that horrible smell?" she said, looking at Dad.

Red Beard gave another roar and pulled a pistol from his belt.

Sammy hid under the table.

"Sammy, what are you doing?" asked Mom. "It's only a thunderstorm!"

Thunder exploded over the house as Red Beard fired his pistol. The first shot went right past Dad's ear and broke the coffeepot.

Mom yelled as Smitty and the pirate crew crashed past her and tried to hide inside the fridge.

The lightning flashed again and Dad jumped to his feet.

Red Beard fired another pistol shot and a cup exploded. Sammy peered out from under the table.

Then something even more amazing happened.

A woman came out of nowhere and stood in the room. She was short and dumpy. She wore a cotton cap and a long apron.

Her face was red and plump and she waved a soup ladle in her hand, like a club.

"Robert Red Beard," she yelled, in a voice that could sink ships.

"Where have you been? You ran off and left me with a whole lot of kids to feed and a house that was falling down. How do you explain that, husband?"

The fridge door opened a crack and Smitty stuck his head out.

He was just in time to see Mrs. Red Beard try to hit her husband with the huge soup ladle.

Red Beard the Really Rotten ran for his life as the little woman chased him out of the kitchen.

"You ran off to sea and left me to a lifetime of hard work and misery!" she yelled after him. "You won't get away from me, you fish-faced sea dog. I'll really get you this time!"

Red Beard the Really Rotten didn't stay around. He forgot all about the pirate crew and revenge.

In a flash, he stomped down the hall at a hundred miles an hour, and was gone forever, with Mrs. Red Beard chasing after him. He left nothing behind but the smell of rotten fish.

Outside, the storm was over and the sun began to shine. Sammy knew that Smitty and the crew would never be bothered by Red Beard again. One by one they came out of the fridge and slipped out of the room.

Mom and Dad busily swept up the mess on the table and floor.

"Phew! I've never seen a storm like that one," Dad said.

Sammy slipped away to his bedroom. Smitty and the pirate crew sat on Sammy's bed, laughing loudly.

"Wasn't it great seeing old Red Beard being chased off like that by his own wife?" asked a pirate.

"She did look mean, didn't she?" said the Squire. "He'll spend the rest of his miserable days keeping out of her way, that's for sure."

The sun shined through the bedroom window as one by one the crew said goodbye and faded into the gray mist.

"Come on, lads. We've got to find a ship," said Boris the officer.

Some pirates went through the walls. Some floated up through the roof. Some faded into the floor.

Crabmeat was the last to go. With one last squawk and one last nuzzle for Polly, he pecked her on the head and vanished.

Sammy felt sad. It had been so exciting having Smitty and his pirate pals around. Now they were all gone.

Polly looked sad, too. She puffed out her feathers and shut her eyes tight.

I should do something for her, Sammy thought.

Then an idea of the perfect thing to do came to him.

He decided that he would clean and polish Polly's cage.

As Sammy began to rub and polish, he suddenly saw a small nameplate on the bottom of the cage.

At first, there didn't seem to be anything written on it.

When Sammy rubbed a bit harder, the name Captain Crabmeat shined through, bright and clear.

Sammy smiled to himself. Now it all made sense. He didn't have to ask Mr. Hackbone after all.

It was Crabmeat's cage which had brought the crazy pirate crew from the other side.

It was Polly who had given the cage a new life.

Sammy carried the cage to his bedroom. From now on, Polly would live there.

"Ahoy there, shipmate!"

Sammy nearly dropped the cage. He spun around. It was Smitty and the pirate crew.

"We think we'll stay after all," they said, grinning. "We thought it might be more fun to hang out here for a while. That is, if there's room on the ship?"

Sammy laughed. "How much room does a ghost pirate crew take up?" he asked.

"Room enough to play a few tricks," Smitty said with a grin. "Now, tell us again about this place called school."

Sammy was happy. He wasn't going to tell anyone about his guests and their adventures.

He was going to keep Smitty and the pirate crew a secret. And he was going to take them to school. What a really cool idea. Dead Cool!

About the Author

Peter Clover keeps a notebook with him all the time, so that whenever an idea hits him he can write it down or draw a picture of it. He lived in Exmoor, England for a time, where he saw a variety of horses. This led him to write and illustrate a highly popular series about an adventurous pony named Sheltie. Clover now lives on the southwestern coast of England, and when he's not busy writing or illustrating he likes to stay in shape. He claims he can still do a back flip while he tosses a pancake in the air.

About the Illustrator

Brann Garvey grew up in the great state of Iowa, where he studied art and visual communications. He graduated from the Minneapolis College of Art & Design with a degree in illustration. Brann is usually found with one or more of the following: a pencil in his hand, a comic book, a remote for watching DVDs, or his pet kitty, Iggy. When the weather is nice, Brann likes to play disc golf, and he proudly points out that Iowa is one of the world's centers for the sport. Iggy does not play.

GLOSSARY

ladle (LAID-uhl)—a long-handled spoon

looming (LOOM-ing)—coming into sight

mascot (MAS-kot)—person, animal, or thing that is supposed to bring luck to a team or group

mutiny (MEW-tun-ee)—a revolt to take control of a ship

pieces of eight (PEE-suz uv ATE)—an old Spanish coin sometimes cut into eight pieces, a favorite of pirates

revenge (ri-VENJ)—to get back or get even with somebody

shifty (SHIFT-ee)—tricky, sneaky

ship ahoy (SHIP a-HOY)—an expression used on a ship to announce the sighting of another ship

shiver me timbers (SHIV-ur ME TIM-burz)—what pirates say when they are scared or surprised

Discussion Questions

1. At the beginning of the book, the author tells us that Sammy wanted a dog more than anything else. Why do you think it was so important to Sammy to have a pet?

2. Throughout the book, only Sammy and Polly can see the pirate crew. Why is it impossible for Sammy's parents to see the crew? How do you think the story would have been different if Sammy's parents had been able to see the visitors?

3. At the end of the story, Sammy plans on taking his pirate friends to school with him. Yet, he also says he's going to keep them a secret. What do you think Sammy wants to happen when he takes his friends to school?

Writing Prompts

1. The pirate crew was invisible to everyone except Sammy. Have you ever wanted to be invisible? Write what you would do if one morning you woke up and found that you were invisible.

2. Describe what might happen to Red Beard the Really Rotten if his angry wife ever really catches up to him.

3. Sammy's experiences with the ghosts started when he bought the parrot. Have you ever bought something that made a big change in your life? What was it? Tell what happened.

ALSO PUBLISHED BY STONE ARCH BOOKS

The Genie
M. Hooper

Fiona discovers that having all her wishes granted by her very own genie might not be as great as she planned. Life gets complicated as soon as she taps on the magic box, calling the genie out.

Living with Vampires
Jeremy Strong

Adam is the only non-vampire in his family. His bloodsucker parents have volunteered to chaperone the school dance. Now Adam needs to make sure his parents don't turn any of his friends into zombies!

Grow up Dad!
Narinder Dhami

A mysterious e-mail grants Robbie's wish: his dad turns into an eleven-year-old kid. Now his dad will see what his life is really like when he faces the school bully!

On the Run
H. Townson

Ronnie hates sports. When he pretends to be sick on Sports Day at his school, Ronnie encounters something much scarier than the high jump.

INTERNET SITES

Do you want to know more about subjects related to this book? Or are you interested in learning about other topics? Then check out FactHound, a fun, easy way to find Internet sites.

Our investigative staff has already sniffed out great sites for you!

Here's how to use FactHound:

1. Visit *www.facthound.com*

2. Select your grade level.

3. To learn more about subjects related to this book, type in the book's ISBN number: **1598891006**.

4. Click the **Fetch It** button.

FactHound will fetch the best Internet sites for you!